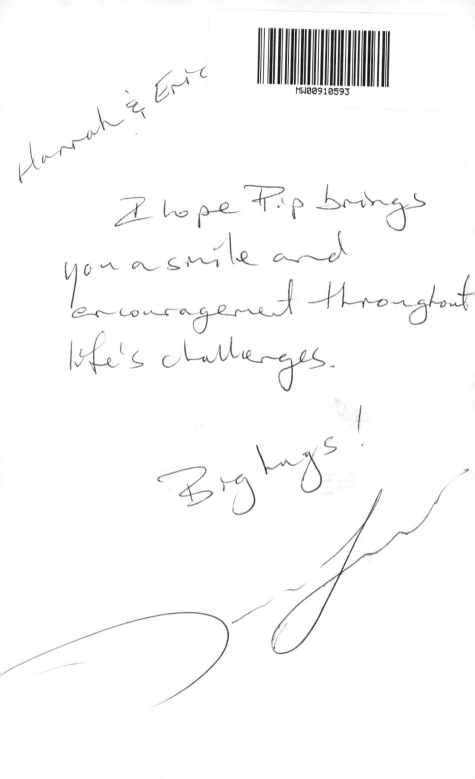

Hannah & Eric

I hope Pip brings
you a smile and
encouragement throughout
life's challenges.

Big hugs!

The Spirited Little Fisherman

"A Pip Adventure"

Dedicated to my family and in memory of my
grandfathers, who lived in a nobler and more
dignified time when a handshake was a man's
word and honor.

It was a cool summer evening in the small New England town of Sandy Hook. It was just cool enough to absorb the heat rising from their skin, tanned from the hot summer beach sun earlier that day. The town was famous for its summer residents who headed there with their families and friends, beach chairs and umbrellas in tow. As dusk set in, the young fisherman, nicknamed Pip for being such a pipsqueak, awaited his turn at the shower. His family's house was packed with every known relative from the Mediterranean to California. He licked the salt from his arm still white with powder from the dried seawater. It reminded him of

pistachios, his favorite nut. It was his turn finally, with only his sister left in line. She always seemed to get the short end of the stick, at least when she was with him. But when she wasn't around he praised her and said she was tops. So in he went, immediately turning on only the cold water. It was so refreshing. He'd dance, splash, and yell at his sister to wait her turn when she demanded that he hurry up. After he was done, he'd throw on a pair of shorts and run out snapping his towel at her.

He was now clean and could relax in comfort on the enclosed veranda watching TV while the women prepared dinner and the men prepared for the big fishing trip the next day. Pip was very excited. They had asked him to go on the big fishing boat. For Pip, an 18 foot power boat was the big fishing boat. In fact, anything that couldn't be thrown on the car's roof was a big boat. He seldom, if ever, was asked to go on the big boats. He was always told that he was too little or there wasn't enough room. He found this strange and always wondered, "Well, if I'm so little, I don't need much room." The gears in his head were always turning. He turned off the TV and

went outside with the older men sitting around the

tackle box. They were predicting the weather,

selecting which bait to buy, and guessing what they

might catch. He would carefully listen to the elders

discuss the tides, the currents, and the line weights

while the middle generation would kick around

soccer balls or pull out a glove and toss a baseball.

His grandfather, whom he much admired, was his

vision of Poseidon's right-hand man.

The call would come from the kitchen and after
ignoring the first three or four cries that dinner was
ready, the men took a seat at the table. It was a
feast of many foods worthy of being served in a fine
restaurant but Pip would have been just as satisfied
with a hotdog. Actually, he might have preferred
one. Dusk turned to dark as the cool sea breeze
crossed the table and rippled the wax on the bottom
of the flat candle holders. Pip loved to play with wax.
He'd drip it on his hand and watch the hot liquid
harden in amazement. But it was different tonight.
He wanted to be excused from the table so that he
could set up his tackle box that was originally his
grandfather's rusty metal toolbox.

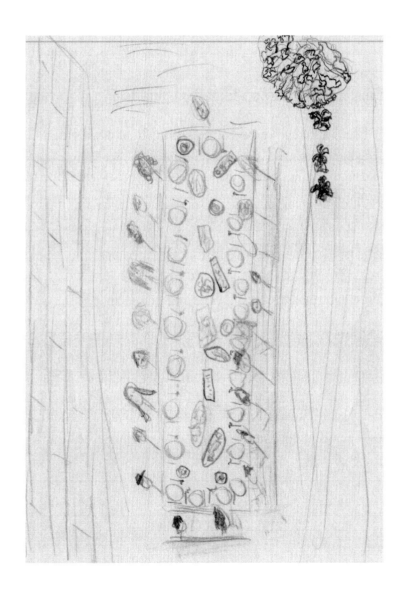

11

This toolbox had special meaning to Pip. He felt it

brought him good luck being that it was his

grandfather's. In the top row of tiny compartments,

he kept his 1, 2, and 3 ounce weights. On the

bottom, the heavier weights, his line, and his hooks.

Pip used a hand line, not a fishing rod. He felt that

by always having his hand on the line, he'd be able

to feel the motion of the fish and not tug too hard. He

saw many fishermen lose their catch by yanking too

hard on their rods.

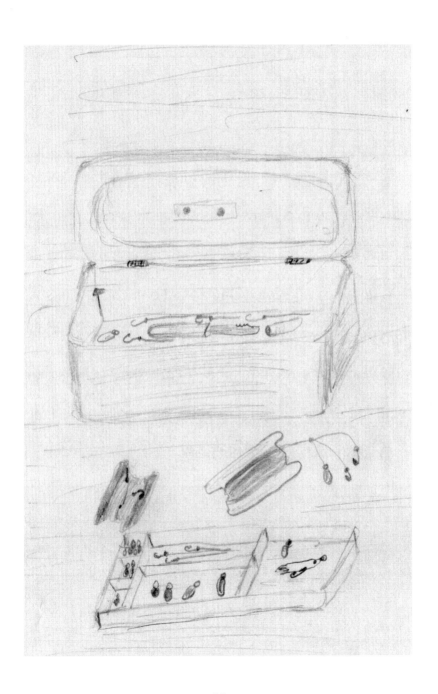

13

The hand line was nothing more than fishing line spooled around a piece of wood hand carved into the shape of a flat hourglass. Beneath the hand lines in a small compartment lay an old bait knife. Pip's favorite bait was the sandworm. He also used squid and clam but always felt that he had the best chance with the sandworm that oozed blood, calling the fish to his hook.

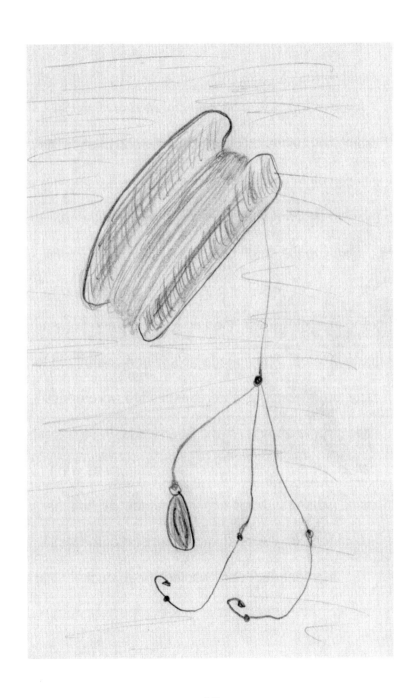

After ensuring that his equipment was in proper order, he brushed his teeth and headed passed the large dining room table, now draped in a green tablecloth. Some had already gathered at the table, shuffling the cards and sipping their cocktail of choice. This was the big after-dinner event. The grand card game that sparked loud conversation and heated topics. The younger folk weren't permitted to play and Monopoly or Parcheesi often covered the "little people table". After a few rounds, Pip's father called him over. Pip sensed something was wrong as he walked towards him. His father told him that someone on the boat invited a friend at the last moment and there wouldn't be enough

room on the boat for him. Pip's eyes began to water but he refused for anyone to see him cry. He would not allow the older group to mock him. He simply said, "That's fine" and walked away. Inside, Pip was disappointed and angry. He felt cheated and useless. He had no desire to continue playing board games and just told everyone that he was tired and wandered off to sleep. He often slept wherever he could on the weekends since the house was full. That night, he slept on an old flat sofa that would be uncomfortable for anyone more than 100 pounds. Pip didn't have to worry about it. He put his face in the pillow and cried quietly so that nobody would hear him.

His mother stopped by just minutes after he went to bed, knowing he was upset. His mother was always there to comfort him and always knew when something was wrong. His pride however, would never let him show his feelings. He told her that he was just tired and the dust from the old couch was bothering his eyes. She kissed his head and wished him goodnight. Pip slowly faded into his pillow dreaming of the fishing trip that would never happen.

Pip awoke with one ear still on his pillow and the other to hushed voices in the other room. At first he couldn't make them out but soon he could tell that these voices were those of the men preparing for that grand fishing trip to be held on the "big boat". Pip didn't wear a watch but he guessed that it was 5 AM since it was still dark outside. He heard footsteps approaching the enclosed porch where he slept and closed his open eye. He knew it was his father. Pip knew his father felt badly so he preferred not to confront him. The footsteps came nearly to the edge of the couch on which he slept and then they turned away after a brief pause. Pip said nothing and fell back to sleep until daylight.

Pip awoke from the clanking of plates in the kitchen.

His grandmother was tidying up the remaining items

from the preceding night.   He heard the women of

the house preparing the dining room table for

breakfast. His mother heard him leave the bathroom

and joined him on the porch. She asked if he wanted

breakfast but Pip wanted no part of it. He wanted to

go fishing. He opened his money jar and pulled out a

few dollars.

His mother asked him where he was going and he told her that he needed to buy sandworms at the bait and tackle shop in town. He hopped on his bicycle, rode to town, and returned to the women preparing their beach bags and lunch. He quickly went hunting for the equipment he'd need for his fishing excursion.

He was taking a boat of his own.

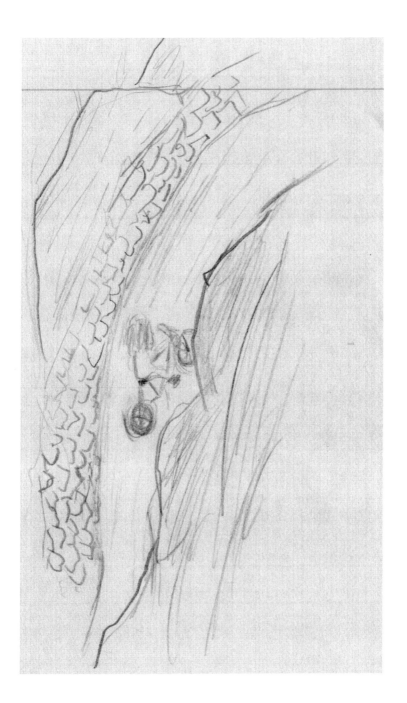

He had a rubber raft that could keep him afloat during his trip, but the tides would take him out quickly, so he needed an anchor. Searching through the basement, he came across some old window weights that he thought would work. He tied two together and then knotted a 30-foot line to the weights. He located a bucket and threw the anchor, the tackle box, and the bait into it. He walked to the shore barefoot so that he wouldn't need to leave his sneakers on the shore. He hated putting on his sneakers with sandy feet. Every few yards he'd step on a pebble sending a painful yet tickling sensation up his leg. The walk wasn't long but hauling the gear made it difficult for Pip.

Crimson Beach was the name of the shoreline where

Pip put his boat in the water. It was here that

residents of Sandy Hook, their family, and friends

took in the sun's rays and swam. Usually, Pip would

be part of that crowd but today, he was on a fishing

adventure. Many of his friends asked where he was

going as did the older folk. Some were eager to

learn of his plan and others doubtful that he'd catch

anything. Pip however, couldn't hang around

chatting as not only did he have fish to catch but the

sand beneath his feet was burning hot. Crimson

Beach was given its name because of the reddish

sand that would become as hot as fire from the

scorching sun.

31

Pip walked to the water and relieved his feet of the scorching sand. He loaded his boat and paddled out into the dark blue water. He headed towards the sandbar since he could always count on catching a crab or two there and pulling in his line from 20 feet was much easier than pulling it in from 40 feet. He never liked a mess in his raft and 40 feet of line without a rod was always a challenge in a one-man float. He dropped his homemade anchor off the side and waited for the gentle feedback from the sandbar. There was a big difference between iron hitting rocks and sand. This difference told Pip when he was on the sandbar.

Pip removed his line from his tackle box and knotted

two new hooks and a weight to it. There was almost

no current so he used a lighter weight. He pulled out

a small chopping board and began cutting up the

sandworms. He carefully put one on each hook. He

dropped in his line and began situating his gear.

Only five seconds after the weight hit bottom, he felt

a nibble. He immediately yanked on the line and

hooked a fish. He was so startled that he knocked

the entire box of sandworms in to the water.

Fortunately, the box was light and filled with seaweed

so he had a few seconds to retrieve it. Once he got

the bait back in the boat, he continued pulling in the

fish. It was a nice size and Pip was confident that it

would be a good day. He filled a quarter of his

bucket with water and dropped in the fish. He was also able to save the piece of bait from the fish's mouth which was always a bonus. He dropped his line again and immediately felt a nibble. He pulled up another. On the next drop, he felt a tug and his line quickly became heavy. He knew immediately that he had a crab. This required a different approach as a crab could easily be yanked off the line. Pip knew he needed to gently pull up the line with a smooth and consistent flow. Sure enough, he had a crab and leftover bait. Down the line went again and another crab clamped its claws to the hook. As Pip began pulling out the line however, he felt the line yanked. He pulled up faster and through the top of the water saw a crab on one hook and a

huge flounder on the other. A double catch! He

hadn't been fishing for five minutes and he had

already caught two fish and two crabs with only one

piece of bait. Pip continued to drop his line and each

time, he'd bring something good up. It was

incredible. His bucket began to fill so he ate his

lunch early and used his lunch bucket for the crabs.

Within a few hours, both were completely filled and

Pip emptied all but a tiny bit of water to keep the fish

cool. He had enough to supply a fish store for the

day.

He pulled up the anchor and began paddling back to the shore with the two heavy buckets in tow off the back of the raft. He was overheated, thirsty, and fatigued yet his excitement over his tremendous catch quashed any pain. He arrived at shore greeted by people eager to see what he had in his buckets. Others on their beach chairs and blankets, curious of the crowd around Pip, came racing over. They couldn't believe how many fish and crabs he had caught. A few people offered to help him but Pip proudly and politely declined. He told them that it was a fishing trip he needed to finish on his own. He hung the inside of the raft on his head and it draped over his back. He then knelt to grab a bucket in each hand. The weight of the buckets with

the anchor and tackle box tied to each was overwhelming but Pip carried on. Today, he was especially thankful that Crimson Beach had a fountain shop. While he'd usually order an egg cream, some rock candy, or an ice cream cone, Pip only wanted water. The heat had gotten to him. It was now time for Pip to begin the tough trek back to the house. Exhausted, overheated, and barefoot, he sprayed his head with water, hoisted the raft over his head, and picked up the buckets. He was off.

Pip made it home, dodging pebbles and hot asphalt,

but it took him four times longer to get back. He was

constantly stopping to give his arms a rest. The

women had already returned from the beach and

were preparing the house for the summer evening

dinner ahead. The men had returned from fishing

and were in the backyard doing their usual thing.

Pip's mother greeted him at the door and asked if he

had caught anything. He didn't respond but simply

removed the rags from the top of the buckets. Her

jaw nearly hit the floor and then she began to gleam.

Pip asked her if his father had caught anything and

she told him, giggling, that the entire boat of men

returned with two tiny fish that wouldn't satisfy his

little sister. She immediately called his father to the

front of the house and told him to look at what his

son had done. His father could only assume that he

had caused some trouble but when he saw them in

front of two buckets smiling, he was puzzled. Pip's

mother removed the rags and smiled. His father was

shocked and thought, "What? How?". Pip just

smirked and turning away said, "Someone has to

feed this family and it doesn't take a big boat to do it."

His dad just rubbed Pip's head and smiled at his

mother as they all went into the house.

The Spirited Little Fisherman
Written and illustrated by Marc Lotti
ISBN 1-932341-00-5